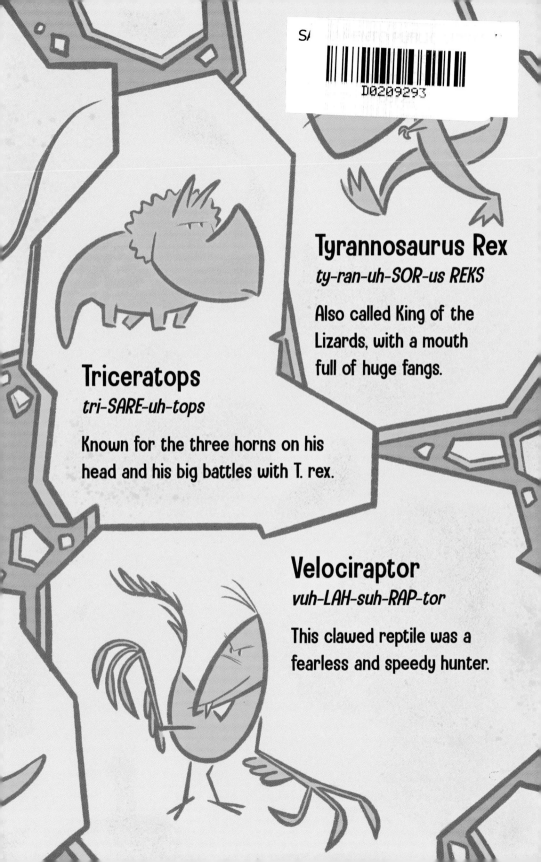

Tyrannosaurus Rex
ty-ran-uh-SOR-us REKS

Also called King of the Lizards, with a mouth full of huge fangs.

Triceratops
tri-SARE-uh-tops

Known for the three horns on his head and his big battles with T. rex.

Velociraptor
vuh-LAH-suh-RAP-tor

This clawed reptile was a fearless and speedy hunter.

Sourcebooks and the colophon are registered trademarks of Sourcebooks.

The full color art was created using Procreate on an iPad Pro.

Published by Sourcebooks Jabberwocky, an imprint of Sourcebooks Kids
P.O. Box 4410, Naperville, Illinois 60567–4410
(630) 961-3900
sourcebookskids.com

Library of Congress Cataloging-in-Publication Data is on file with the publisher.

Source of Production: Worzalla, Stevens Point, Wisconsin, USA
Date of Production: June 2022
Run Number: 5025314

Printed and bound in United States of America
WOZ 10 9 8 7 6 5 4 3 2 1

Tea Time for DINOSAURS

A. J. Smith

sourcebooks
jabberwocky

Raging raptors!
Soaring pterosaurs!
It was a time of terror...

A time of trumpets
and tutus.

Umm...
No.

Tops wasn't like
other triceratops.

Tyra wasn't like
other T. rexes.

None of the other dinosaurs liked this.

Tyra and Tops loved dancing.
They loved music.

And they loved doing
them together!

But Tyra's dad said...

Tyra and Tops had an idea!
They invited the other
dinosaurs to a tea party,
with music and dancing.

The other dinosaurs had never seen a tea party.

So, they did what they always do...

When it was all over,

Tyra's tutu was

TATTERED.

And Tops had a
TRAMPLED TRUMPET.

They wanted to rage.
They wanted to...

It did feel good to impress everyone!

NOPE.

NO
MORE!

The other dinosaurs were quiet for a moment.

The dinosaurs got to work, using their skills.

Plesiosaur
PLEE-zee-uh-sor

This ~~rapid reptile~~ master chef was a wiz in the ~~water.~~ kitchen.

Megazostrodon
MEG-uh-ZOS-tro-don

One of the first mammals, he ~~was~~ became a sneaky scavenger, of cupcakes and cookies.

Pterosaur
TEHR-uh-sor

This winged lizard was the biggest animal that ever ~~flew.~~ carpenter swung a hammer.

Spinosaurus
SPY-nuh-SOR-us

Also called the ~~"spine lizard"~~ seamstress ~~because of the big, spiny sail~~ ~~on its back.~~ he enjoyed making mittens and blankets.